AF235877

Three Witches

Love Wild

Bibliografische Information der Deutschen Nationalbibliothek:

Die Deutsche Nationalbibliothek verzeichnet diese Publikation in der Deutschen Nationalbibliografie; detaillierte bibliografische Daten sind im Internet über http://dnb.dnb.de abrufbar.

Herstellung und Verlag: BoD – Books on Demand, Norderstedt

ISBN: 978-3-7526-3900-1

I.

Life in the countryside was often considered boring by the people who lived in cities. They weren't wrong. There's almost nothing to do here, and the most exciting days were the ones where we would go into the city to sell our crops and other goods. Luckily, I live near two other farms and have friends that I've known since I was a kid. We did everything together, from hiding to avoid field work to camping out in one of our barns together. We were always look for something new and exciting to do, which didn't come often. so when we found something really old and interesting, we learned all we could about it. My name is Mary Bixby and me and my friends made an amazing find.

II.

It was the beginning of fall and I had my two friends, Amelia and Virginia, over in my family's barn. All of our parents were pretty strict when it came to having guests over. It would be less irritating if we were all still kids, but we weren't. I'm the oldest out of all of us and I'm twenty years old, Amelia is nineteen, and Virginia had just turned eighteen. Since we still lived in our families' houses, we lived by their rules. That's why we often found ourselves in the barns. We weren't Amish or anything, but we still wore conservative dresses that covered us from neck to ankles. Let me tell you, those are awful in the summer.

We were all talking in the barn as we sat in the hay and giggled about the cute city boys we met while we were in town throughout the week. Though, really, it was just me and Amelia talking to each other while Virginia sat there quietly, clutching onto her satchel. "I think his name was Jason! Isn't that cute?" Amelia grinned and bounced in her seat. Okay, it wasn't hard to get us going. Farm life could be just that boring and we lived nowhere near the other farms that had the handsome fieldhands.

I leaned in and took ahold of Amelia's hands and squeezed them. "What'd he look like?" I asked eagerly. This was a time where I was definitely innocent and loved to gossip about silly things like boys.

Amelia sighed with a dreamy expression. She looked to Virginia and quirked a brow. "Hey! What're ya doin' mopin' over there?" She reached past me which pressed her impressive breasts against mine with a squish. Oh, if only I knew then what I know now. I would have enjoyed it more. Amelia took Virginia by her wrist and tugged her towards us. "C'mon!"

Virginia gasped and fell forward. she still held onto that satchel as if it was made of glass! "I, uh…" She sat up and composed herself as she looked between us. "I found something." Her voice was soft like she was whispering to a mouse even though no one else was around.

I looked at her funny and tilted my head. "Found somethin'?" Then my eyes went to her satchel and before she could react, I snatched it up. "This?" I dangled her satchel away from her with a playful grin.

But she didn't find anything playful about it at all! "Wait! Give that back, Mary!" She pleaded and grabbed for it. She ended up in my lap as she pouted at me. Another missed opportunity due to my ignorance.

I finally handed the satchel back to her and pursed my lips. "What's in it, then?"

Amelia scooched in closer and smiled with excited interested.

"It's… a book." Virginia murmured. She had shoulder length blonde hair that she always kept in a tight bun and with how mousy she was, you'd think she really was Amish. She was so quiet and nervous all the time. We always had to convince her to do something new because she was worried about getting in trouble or getting hurt.

Amelia gave her a flat expression. "A book?" She sighed in exasperation. "You're the only one who likes readin' that much, Virginia."

She picked up some hay and tossed it at the timid girl.

The sweet blonde pouted as she remained in my lap. I was only three years older than her but she really did act like a little sister. Though, after a moment, she took said book out of her satchel and held it up to me. It looked really old. The cover was made out of leather it looked like and the pages weren't normal book paper we have nowadays. "B-be careful." She cautioned me.

I opened the book up and the pages were filled with manual hand writing. The language was definitely English but it looked like a fairly old version of it. As I thumbed through these pages, I gasped and stuffed the book back into the satchel. "Virgnia! This book's about witchcraft!" I took the satchel from her and sat it to the side after nudging her off of my lap.

Amelia took immediate interest and sntached up the pack then removed the book from its holdings. "Witchcraft?" She echoed and opened it up. Her eyes lit up as she read along the pages and she bit her bottom lip. "This is so cool, you guys! Like, this seems like the real deal!" She squealed. When she finally looked up, she seemed to note my look of terror and Virginia's own subdued curiosity. "Oh, c'mon. What? Ya can't tell me it's not interesting? What if a real witch wrote this? It's… it's historical!" She insisted.

I shook my head and reached to grab for the book again. "It's the Devil's words, Amelia!" I missed as she pulled away from me and got to her feet.

"Ya can't be serious. It's not that bad! Look! Uh… this page says somethin' about bein' able to heal wounds and stuff! Maybe it was a good witch that wrote it!" Amelia still skimmed through the book and grimaced once. "Okay, well, not all of it is good. But, uh… look here!" She pointed to a page she found and motioned us over to her. "In any case wherein there is good and evil there must remain a balance. One curse undone requires once more a curse fulfilled." She quoted the book and furrowed her brow in thought. "So, it sounds like whoever this woman was, she was probably good! It just says, uh… that even though there are good spells to undo evil curses, there's gotta be bad curses because of "balance".

As she spoke, both me and Virginia looked at her in shock. That was probably the easiest passage to read in the book when it came to the structure of the language, and she seemed to pick it up so easily. When she explained it to us, I started to believe it! It made sense, after all. Even in Sunday school we were taught that there's always good and evil and one cannot be without the other. The same theory applied to these curses and such. Was it really so bad if someone used these powers for good? "Ah, Amelia…" I bit my bottom lip as I looked to her with uncertainty. "We should just keep this between us. Ya know?"

She nodded vigorously. "Obviously! Our parents would be so mad! And we don't wanna get burned at the stake." She winked, obviously kidding since nothing like that had been legal practice for… well, maybe a couple of centuries.

The mention of being burned at the stake made Virginia jump a little and she held onto the back of my dress. "Maybe I should put it back!' She squeaked.

I turned to her and kissed her cheek. "It'll be fine. I promise. I doubt we can do anything anyway. But it'll be neat to read, won't it?"

The younger girl looked up at me and sighed softly. "Yeah, I already read some. … it's interesting." She managed a smile and straightened her dress out.

Amelia was engrossed in the book again so I snapped my fingers to get her to pay attention. "We can take turns havin' it when we're not together. And since you're so attached to it right now, I guess you can take it first." I pouted a little because I'd really like to read it. I didn't want an argument with Amelia, though. I might have been the oldest but she always won. She was a fighter! It made sense, really. She was 5'8" and had a sturdy frame, not to mention those luscious breasts. She could throw a punch as good as any farmhand could. Her hair was even longer than Virginia's. The raven colored tresses went down to her waist and she allowed the wavy locks to flow freely. Out of the three of us, she had the least strict parents. Her dress also seemed too small for her figure as her breasts were boasting heavy cleavage up top.

When it came to Virginia, she was petite and frail. Amelia and I might tussle sometimes, but neither of us would lay a hand on little Virginia. I was in the middle of the road with an average body, including modest breasts, and bright red hair that only reached to my chin. The pair were jealous of my deep green eyes, though!

Amelia took Virginia's satchel and stuffed the book back inside of it. "Well, I'm gonna go home before it gets dark. I'm sure momma's gonna have dinner ready soon." she grinned and waved to us by wiggling her fingers. "Maybe I'll see ya'll tomorrow." She teased. Then again, I was sure she would stay inside with that book as long as she could.

III.

Later that night after supper, I was lying in bed in my thin white nightgown but I couldn't get the thought of the strange book out of my head. I wish I hadn't been so nice and let Amelia have it first. All I wanted to do was read it and find out what all it said. What kind of spells did it hold? Would there be love spells? I blushed a little at the thought of that. There were a few boys I'd met that I wanted to be more than friends with, but I never knew how to approach them and they certainly never asked me. My thoughts eventually lulled me to sleep at some point. I vaguely remembered some of the dreams I had, and they were all about my final thoughts before falling asleep. Love spells. That's what I was interested in.

IV.

I awoke that morning and I felt more tired than I was before I went to bed. My dreams had wreaked havoc on my mind and made me restless. I needed that book! I quickly dressed myself in one of my many dresses and combed my hair. These locks are untameable, though so it was still fluffed out and a bit messy. My red strands framed my face nicely, though, so I couldn't complain about that.

I made my way downstairs and my parents were already eating breakfast. My father looked up at me and quirked a brow. "Mary…" He cleared his throat and beckoned me over.

I walked over to him and smiled brightly. While my father was strict, he wanted us to remain smiling as often as possible. A frown could be a sign of disrespect. I never said my family was normal. Maybe being around so much corn made people a little strange. I stopped beside him with my hands clasped in front of my body against my dress, and I lean down to kiss his cheek. "Good morning, daddy."

He returned the smile and kissed my cheek, as well. "Morning, sweetheart. I see you can sleep through the day if your mother or I don't wake you." He raised a brow at me and continued eating his breakfast. He clearly wanted an explanation. It was expected of us to wake up on our own after a certain age. According to my father, that age was four. 'We have alarm clocks, after all', he would always say. There might have been times where I purposely didn't set my alarm.

I was intent on going to Amelia's house, but I slipped to the side where my place was set and had food waiting. After plopping down into the chair, I began eating before saying anything. "Well… me, Amelia, and Virginia were out playing all day." I said innocently enough. Though, it was a little strange for a twenty year old to say she was "playing", but father didn't like the term "hanging out" much. "I suppose I was tired and didn't think to set my alarm."

"Uh-huh. Think ahead next time, Mary. It isn't becoming for you to sleep in so late." He grunted then went back to his food after giving a glance to my mother that I noted.

She smiled to me and nodded. "Your father's right, Mary. You'll develop bags beneath your eyes by sleeping like that." She was being a bit playful, but she always did say, "What man wants to marry a tired woman?" And there it was.

I chuckled even though I was rolling my eyes on the inside. Ugh. I wasn't interested in marrying. I just wanted to date and have some fun with the boys, but my mother would have a stroke if I told her any of that. "You're right. I'll be better about it." I smiled to both of them and continued eating. The rest of the meal was finished in silence. Being the good daughter that I am, I got up and gathered up the plates, placing them in the sink.

"Going out today, honey?" My mother asked with a sweet voice. She had gotten up, as well, and my father had already left the room to go about his morning routine.

I turn and look at her with a smile. This one was genuine. "Uh huh. Gonna go over to

Amelia's. Maybe go to the city if her family's takin' a trip." Of course, I was going over there to take possession of the book. The need for it was gnawing at me and nearly driving me crazy with curiosity.

"Oh, alright. Be safe and come back before ten tonight." She said so casually as if I was no older than twelve. I really needed to start making my own money.

"Yes, ma'am!" I called to her, already walking toward the front door where a pair of my shoes were. I slipped them on and hurried out of the door. I grabbed my bike from the side of the house and hopped on. With these annoying dresses, I had to be careful and adjust the fabric so it wouldn't get caught while avoiding it getting hiked up and looking indecent. The last thing I needed was other people talking to my father about how I looked like a harlot riding a bike. The people around here are ridiculous.

I got to Amelia's after about five minutes and parked by bike off to the side of the porch. I landed my hand against the door heavily three times. It took about twenty seconds or so but her older sister answered the door. Seeing the way that she was allowed to dress, I was reminded on how lenient their parents were. She had the same raven hair as Amelia, but she had it cut short and spiked with purple highlights. She wore a pair of jean shorts and a white tank top that didn't do much to hide her abundant assets. She always made me blush and feel a little shy. If I had been less sheltered, I would have realized why I felt like that. Alas.

"Oh, hey, Mary." She said casually and stepped aside. "Amy's upstairs." Only her family called her "Amy". If I started to, I might slip up in front of my parents or Virginia's and call her that myself. It was considered indecent to shorten given names like that. Everything was indecent, apparently.

"Thanks, Catherine!" I squeaked out with a bright smile as I stepped inside.

She sighed and scoffed. "It's Cat." She insisted in a droll voice. Yet another name I didn't dare shorten.

So I just nodded to her and waved as I headed upstairs to Amelia's room. I knocked on her door twice and received no answer. She didn't open it and she didn't call for me to come in or even stay out. How rude! I knocked once more and heard a faint, "Uh huh…"

I opened the door at that and walked in, then closed it behind me. "Amy?" I cooed in a teasing manner since she knew I never called her that. I chuckled a little but when I saw her, I jumped. She looked completely exhausted! Her hair was messy and while she wasn't in her same dress, she just wore her panties. Before I turned away, I saw the book between her legs as she sat there. It looked like she was near the middle of it. I quickly turned away and cleared my throat. "Uh..."

I don't know if she looked up at me, but she did speak. "Oh, hey, Mary." She said as if it was the most normal thing in the world that she was naked on her bed reading a book on witch-craft.

"Uh, Amelia? Have you... slept?" I questioned in concern. I also felt a strange tingle

27

along my body. My nipples pressed against my dress. The bust of the dress provided support so I didn't have to wear a bra with it, but the fabric didn't hide much in times like that.

"Huh? Oh, no. I've been readin' this book. It's amazin' stuff, Mary. C'mere." She insisted and I felt like I could sense her gaze on me now.

"O-okay. But shouldn't ya get a little dressed? Heh." I was trying to sound light-hearted as if I didn't care.

She scoffed. "Just c'mere." Her voice was more serious and it sounded like a com-mand. "Ya know... I read about a spell that can control a person briefly. Don't make me use it." She was teasing me, but then again it felt like she'd do it if she could.

I quickly turned and looked at her with concern. "Haha, real funny." I said back as I walked over to her and sat on the other side of the bed. I bit my bottom lip and kept my attention on the book.

She glanced over to me and giggled. "I can see your hard nipples, Mary. What, did the sight of my sister get you wet again?"

I couldn't believe what she said. I had never said anything about her sister before. "What?" I gasped out and blushed deeply.

"Uh huh. I see the way ya look at her. Ya probably don't get it, though. I always knew ya liked girls even if ya don't believe it yourself. It'd be real shameful, huh?" She grinned and pushed the book to the side and crawled over to me.

My eyes went to her body finally and I made a soft sound even I didn't understand. "I... what? Amelia! What's gotten into ya?"

She reached out and stroked her fingers over my covered nipples. They got even more stiff and sensitive as she touched them and I couldn't pull away from her. "Mn? Nothin' at all. I've always thought you're pretty, Mary. And I was readin' this book all night. It says a lot about sisterhood and... enjoyin' one another. It helps power the magic." She leaned into to me and kissed my cheek lightly.

Her lips felt like a feather tickling my skin. "M-magic? Amelia, ya can't... I mean you're not... " She wasn't a witch! What was she going on about like she understood? My breath had become a bit heavier and I whimpered softly.

"We can. Me, you, Virginia…" She murmured and reached up, stroking my cheek gently. "Doesn't it feel right? We can actually be somethin', Mary! Instead of borin' farm girls. Isn't this what we've been waitin' for?"

"I mean, well…" I wasn't very good with words at the time and I was terribly aroused by my own best friend! "It'd be interestin'…" I admitted softly and closed my eyes.

"Then don't act so silly!" She giggled and suddenly her lips were against mine. She was kissing me! And it was long. Her fingers stroked over my nipples still and she forced my lips apart with her tongue to push it inside. The kiss was messy since we were both new to it and we were both moaning softly. "Oh, Mary… only Cat's home. Let's have some fun for once." She cooed and pushed into me, forcing my legs open so she could be between them. "I'm tired of just touchin' myself at night. I came at least seven times last night and this mornin'. I'm just so horny." She licked at my lips softly.

"Amelia…" I breathed out and leaned back against one of the bed posts. I felt faint and and lightheaded as my slit between my legs throbbed and my nipples rubbed against the fabric of my dress.

"I'll make ya feel good." Amelia grinned and tugged down the top of my dress to expose my breasts. "Mn, so cute, Mary. They're smaller than mine. Only Virginia has smaller tits, but I like them this way." She was clearly eager and I never heard her speak like that!

I pouted a little and bit my bottom lip lightly. "Don't say that, Amelia. It's mean…" I protested in embarrassment. I was always jealous that my breasts weren't as big as hers. Mine were incredibly sensitive, though, so what she did next made me cry out.

She used the long, wet flat of her tongue to lick over my nipple and flick it a few times while her other hand teasingly rolled my lonely nipple beneath her fingertip. She looked up at me all the while as she toyed with my little buttons. After a few licks, she started sucking on my nipple firmly and moaning against it in need. "It's not mean... I love your breasts, Mary." She moved her head and placed her head between my breasts! She nuzzled against them and licked slowly over the flesh. Both of her hands busied themselves with tugging at and squeezing my nipples. "Am I makin' your panties wet?" She giggled.

I couldn't lie to her. I didn't want to. "Y-yeah... I can feel them clingin' to my lips." I admitted softly to her. I spread my legs more and even tugged my dress up to show her my white panties. They were clearly damp over my slit and the outlines of my lips were easy to see.

She finally released my breasts, now slick with her saliva, and leaned back to look at me. "Ohh, yes." Amelia reached down and slowly stroked her fingers over the middle of my panties, making them rub against me. She found the little button that's my clit and began stroking over that specifically. "Is this how ya touch yourself?"

I nodded. "R-right there. I rub right there." There was no going back. I loved every moment of her touch as I sat there with my dress up and my legs spread, my breasts spilling from the top of my dress.

"And…" She slowly tugged my panties to the side and groaned softly. "Fuck. Oh, Mary." She moaned and stroked her fingers over my bare lips. "Your pussy is so cute! So pink!" She gasped and found my clit once more. Her fingers found a way to get the hood of my clit out of the way and she was rubbing it directly.

"I like when ya talk like that." I moaned out and reached up to the bedpost, feeling the need to hold onto it as she made me squirm. Unexpectedly, my pussy squirted a little and got onto Amelia's palm. "Oh! Gah…"

She grinned at me and lifted her palm up to show me how sticky it was. "Makin' a mess, Mary." She teased me then pressed her fingers to my lips. "Let's taste ya." She leaned in and kissed me again while working a finger against my lips.

I returned the kiss and also tasted myself on her finger with her. We moaned together and her bare breasts were pressed against mine now. Her nipples slipped against mine, making me cry out sharply. "Amelia…" I licked her finger and sucked on the tip. "I'm makin' such a mess on your bed."

"That's right. I came all over it a lot tonight." She grinned again and sat back to get a good look at me. "Ah, ya look like a whore." She bit her bottom lip. She reached down and spread my pussy with her fingers, dipping her middle finger inside. "So tight!" Even though she said that, she worked in a second!

I arched my back and bucked my hips a little. "Oh, wait!" I gasped in surprise. I didn't often use my fingers inside of myself, and Amelia had a whole different angle on me than I did when I touched myself. I didn't try to stop her, though. It felt amazing. I was just embarrassed that I enjoyed it so much.

Of course, she didn't wait. She continued to finger me as she giggled and moaned softly. She was enjoying it for more than just sexual pleasure. I could tell she was enjoying my insincere protests as she made me squirm and whimper. Then she reached back to my ankle and jerked on it suddenly, forcing me onto my back with my legs up in the air. "There we go..." She purred and with my hips and legs up, she leaned down and her tongue started to lap at my pussy without hesitation.

I bit my bottom lip again and whimpered. The feeling was incredible! I was so sticky and wet that I wanted to tell her to stop. It was so dirty to let her lick up all of that lewd arousal. But she did so with enthusiasm and moaned as if I was the one tasting her like that. I gripped the sheets and tilted my head back. "Amelia… this is… we can't!" I insisted, but I also spread my legs more.

"Do ya mean that? Your pussy's practically a fountain." She teased and let my legs down. After she did that, she tugged her own panties down and off. "Here, I'm still sticky with my cum from earlier." She murmured and scooched forward, keeping me pinned down. Before I knew it, she was over my face and her arousal was dripping onto my lips. "Tell ne if a need air." She giggled once more and lowered herself so her swollen pussy lips were against my lips. She really did work herself raw.

I couldn't help myself. My tongue slipped from my lips and lapped over her in need. I pressed my tongue up and felt it actually touch her inner walls a bit. "Nn…" I moaned against her and started suckling on her lips as well, giving them small tugs which she seemed to enjoy. She bucked against me each time I suckled on her pussy lips. I also reached up and found her clit. I was going to make her squirm like she made me! I tugged up the little hood of her clit and sucked on the little button directly. She squirted into my mouth! "Mm!" I lapped up the juices. Then I felt her touch on my once more.

She was pushing her fingers into my slit and using them to finger me hard. She was thrusting against my face and made it hard to breathe. "Oh, yes! Mary! Lick my pussy!" She cried out as she bucked against me. Her fingers thrust deep inside of my and she was going harder and harder. I felt myself close to my breaking point. Right before I nearly screamed, I felt her wetness pour onto my face as she squirted heavily and pushed down roughly to make sure I also drank as much as I could.

That's what was too much for me. Feeling her climax against my face made me arch my back as I came hard and squirted as well. This was the first I'd ever done something like that and I couldn't believe how incredible it felt! I could feel my insides twitching and throbbing as I went through my heavy orgasm until I was lying back and limp. Her pussy was still against my mouth and I gave it a few soft licks and a sigh. "Gosh…"

Amelia groaned and slowly slipped away. She was purposefully dragging her pussy down my body and making it sticky. She grinned at me and kissed me. "Mn, we've started a lovely sisterhood, Mary." She cooed. "Feelin' ecstasy like that's part of bein' a witch. Are ya still up for it?" She looked into my eyes as our bodies pressed against each other.

Feeling her nipples slip against mine was enough to solidify my decision. 'Y-yeah. I am." I nodded and smiled faintly.

"Good." She kissed me deeply again and lightly stroked her fingers over my messy slit. "Get decent. Let's go get, Virginia."

V.

After we get toweled off and dressed, we headed over to our friend's home. We both knocked on the door a couple times, knowing that her parents weren't home since their car was gone. It didn't take long for Virginia to answer. She smiled brightly when she opened the door. "Oh! Hello, you two!" She squeaked out and stepped out of the door, closing it behind her. "I wasn't expecting either of you today." She glanced to Amelia and giggled. "I can't believe Mary got you away from that book!"

Amelia grinned and took a step forward. "Oh, she found a way." She cooed.

My eyes widened and I nudged Amelia away from Virginia. That book really had changed her somehow. I didn't expect her to be so forward with our innocent friend. Hopefully she didn't notice. "Anyway. Amelia thinks she found a way to do some of the stuff in the book. But a lot of it takes at least three people."

Amelia nodded. "Yeah, for power and all that." She said casually as if she knew everything there was to know about it. She was still eyeing the poor girl in a strange manner.

"Do some of it? Perform… witchcraft?" Virginia squeaked out and shifted on her feet. "I-I was just reading it. I never intended to…"

"Well, we do." Amelia interrupted the stammering girl. "So, are ya gonna help us? What if we die 'cause ya weren't there to help?" She folded her arms and gave the young girl a look that always made her fold like a house of cards.

"Amelia! Geeze." I sighed out and shook my head. Before I could say anymore to defend little Virginia, she spoke up.

"O-okay." She said softly and bit her bottom lip. "But we can't do anything bad. Okay?"

Amelia grinned, quite pleased with herself. I never tried to manipulate our friend like she always did. Though, I was always a little impressed that it continually worked over the years. i couldn't think of a time where Virginia actually ever told Amelia no. "Alright, let's go to your family's barn since they're not home anyway. Ya know, in case anything goes boom." She laughed and started to lead the way to the barn not too far off in the distance.

"Boom?" The younger girl looked at me with wide eyes and I just nudged her to follow alongside me as Amelia led the way.

"There won't be any "boom"." I assured her and shook my head.

Once we got to the barn, Amelia closed the doors behind us and brought out the book. "Okay! What should we do first?" She sat down on the ground and started flipping through the pages.

Virginia and I both sat, as well, with the youngest girl between us. She looked over at the book and tilted her head. "Well, what all does it have? If it even does work…" She bit her bottom lip.

Amelia didn't say anything for a few moments, then she stopped on a page and placed her finger on it. "Here we go! I'm sure this one would work!" As Virginia leaned in to take a look, our oldest friend tugged her in with one arm as her other hand suddenly went to her modest breasts and groped them.

"A-Amelia!" She gasped out in shock and embarrassment. She was squirming to push away but Amelia had a strong grip on her smaller body.

"Hold on now, look!" She keeps stroking and groping the writhing girl's breasts as she brought her attention to what she was reading/ "A body enhancement spell! Probably to make people bigger or smaller, but it looks like we can just do body parts, too." She grins and clearly got a grip on Virginia's nipple as she tugged on it. "They're so little, Ginny. Don't ya want 'em bigger?"

The young girl's face was flushed a dark red and she whimpered. "Stop it, Amelia! I... I don't want them to be bigger." She huffed insistently.

Amelia released the girl's breast and we could easily see her stiff nipples pressed against the fabric of her dress. She wore something lighter today so the fabric wasn't oppressive. "But they'd look so cute! C'mon, do it for me? I'm only doin' what's best for ya. Won't find a husband with such small breasts."

"Ya can't say things like that!" I insisted with an angry glare. "She'd-" I halted my words when our new keeper of the book narrowed her eyes at me.

"Mind your own business, Mary. I know our cute girl here would like some more assets! Right, Ginny?" Amelia stroked the girl's cheek lightly and smiled ever so sweetly.

"I... w-well. Alright. Just a little! I mean... if it even works! It probably won't." It sounded like she was trying to assure herself more than she didn't believe that the spell would work. Then again, none of us had a reason to believe all of this was anything but nonsense. I thought.

"Oh, it will! I tried a few simple things last night. I guess I'm gifted." Amelia said with such smugness, I believed her. She placed her hand against her chest and her eyes fluttered as if she was trying to charm someone.

"What did you do?" I asked in a gasp.

She shook her head. "That's not important. What's important is getting our little Ginny here equipped with some luscious breasts." She giggled and nudged the smaller girl. "Gotta take your shirt off, silly. What if it does work and you bust outta your clothes?"

She blinked and tilted her head. "Gee, I don't think it would be that bad." She murmured but nodded. What if they got all squished and constricted? The nervous girl was shaking a little but removed her dress. Her movements were tentative and slow until it was up and off and she dropped it to the floor. She wore simple white panties and some stockings. Her breasts weren't big enough yet to need a bra and she was eighteen! She placed her arms over them and stared down at the ground.

"Ah-ah, silly!" Amelia chided again. "Don't cover 'em up, we need 'em!" When she got her arms away from her chest, she shamelessly caressed her fingertips over the girl's little nipples. They became stiff quickly and Virginia whimpered. "Oh, don't worry, Ginny. This is just a preparation." She cooed. I wasn't sure if she was lying or not, but I didn't want to question her again. There was something about the new Amelia that made me uneasy.

Virginia moaned softly and bit her bottom lip as Amelia toyed with her nipples. "O-okay. It feels... nice, though." She wiggled a little and tilted her head back.

The older girl was having way too much fun with her friend's reactions and began to tug on her little nipples before she let them go. "Mn, okay. So... this one. I just have to say these words and put power behind them. She began to read off of the page in an olde English that included words that had to be in another language. As she did, her hands reached out to grasp both of Virginia's bare breasts. She lightly rubbed her palms against them and repeated the long string of words over and over. A very faint purple light encircled her hands and then covered the young girl's breasts!

I opened my mouth to say something, completely in shock. I refrained, though. I had no idea what was going on or what could happen if I interrupted whatever Amelia was doing. Clearly something was happening. I just watched in awe as the apparent magic started to envelop my innocent friend. The scary part was that it did look like Amelia had some sort of inherent talent for this. It couldn't be easy to just pick up a spellbook and start practicing magic!

The young girl that was the target of the spell looked down at herself with wide eyes. It looked like she wanted to escape but was frozen in place. She was always a sweet, wholesome girl. Witchcraft or anything of the like was a frightening tale to her, yet here she was. Her chest rose and fell heavily and after a few moments, her breasts slowly became visibly bigger and swelled in size. They were growing large enough that they forced Amelia's fingers to spread out around them to be able to hold them. After a few more minutes of gradual growing, our new witch stopped casting the spell and Virginia was left with what had to be DDD breasts. She looked down at herself in shock and began to cry! "I-I can't believe…! This was so wrong, Amelia!"

The newly awakened witch released the young woman's breasts and eyed her hungrily. "Wrong? Aren't they great? Might have to buy some new clothes, but… won't have trouble finding a man. And aren't your parents already on you about findin' someone to marry?" She chuckled. "You just look more like a woman now." The frightened girl was still crying as Amelia spoke, so the witch leaned in and kissed her lips softly. "Shh, shh. It'll be fine. Here, I'll show ya how they can make ya feel."

I still sat on the sidelines, speechless. Before my eyes this small chested girl had grown bigger than even me! Her nipples looked so softly that I wanted to suck on them and give them firm licks. I shook my head and discarded such thoughts. Amelia was one thing but little Virginia?! Then again, Amelia seemed to have no trouble with manipulating the girl to fit her needs. She gently laid the big breasted beauty down onto the hay on the ground and made sure she had her arms over her head to stretch her body up a bit. Virginia's enormous breasts bounced and swayed as she moved and was positioning on the floor.

"A-Amelia, what are you doing?" She murmured out with such a cute pout on her lips.

In response, our older friend sat beside her and laid on her side. "Makin' you enjoy these, Ginny. We need to... break them in." She giggled at that and started to kiss over one of the girl's breasts. Her lips trailed along until she got the the nipple and gave placed a soft kiss on it. After noting how the innocent farmgirl shuddered and whimpered, she began sucking on the little button as her other hand grabbed another big tit. She groped and squeezed firmly as her head lifted up to tug on her nipple with her lips before letting go with a pop. "Mm, these are amazin', sweetheart. I wonder if your little pussy is wet..."

The lewd word caused Virginia to sit up a little but with Amelia over her like that she had to spread her legs to steady herself. "You can't say something like that, Amelia!" She gasped. Her cheeks were flushed red and she looked terribly embarrassed again.

Amelia quirked a brow and reached below the young girl's waist and up her thighs. It was clear her fingers had met their destination, because it got a gasp from Virginia and she spread her legs more. "I can't?" The young witch finally answered as she stroked her fingers along Virginia's panties.

"W-why do I feel like this? I'm so hot, and... ah... don't do that, Amelia. You're getting my panties all dirty." She pouted and looked between her legs. I was surprised that even loyal Virgnia wasn't protecting what Amelia was doing until the touchy woman spoke.

"Don't worry, Ginny. I just added a little… oomf to the spell. To make ya more perceptive to my touch. I wouldn't want to have to pin ya down." She giggled and tugged the panties to the side. "What a tight little pussy. Even more than Mary's!"

"Amelia!" I gasped, both flustered and a little insulted. I also had the guts to say something finally. "How did you do that, too?" I question and lower my gaze, feeling too subdued to look this new woman in the eyes.

Now her fingers stroked over Virginia's pink lips as the older girl looked to me. "Oh, I should've said something, I guess! I was readin' up on old family history… mostly the books mom and dad keep locked away for some reason. Looks like that reason is that we have some witches back in the family tree and my parents are so damn superstitious and shit that they hid it from me. So..." Her middle finger squishes into the girl's little slit, making her cry out and lie back again. "I had some talent all along that needed unlockin'."

"Nnn! Yes, Amelia! Touch me more... I-I love this." The nearly naked girl on the ground was squirming with her legs spread wide now. Her own hands were toying with her huge breasts, rubbing over her nipples and tugging on them eagerly as they became stiff and swollen with arousal.

I'm still taken aback by the scene, but I start to rub myself over my panties and dress as I watch them. The influence Amelia had over Virginia was humbling. She was always the leader of our trio, but now it was as if she was solidifying her position and making us submissive to her. I caught a glance from the very confident woman and she grinned at me as she added another finger inside of the writhing girl beneath her. "Amelia, wait… we shouldn't-" I murmured and bit my bottom lip when her hand slipped away from the large breasted young girl, and she held it up to show how sticky and messy her fingers were.

"Mn? What do ya want, Mary? Ah, what about that boy in town… Tyler?" She giggled and slid down between Virginia's legs as she spoke. "Gettin' him to be attracted to ya's a pretty simple spell, actually. Though…" She gives her partner's pussy lips a light kiss and starts sucking on them gently. "Mn, though it takes some physical components." Between speaking, she suckled on Virginia's lips and toyed with her little clit. "They're not hard to get, though."

"Amelia! P-please push your tongue in. It's so warm… s-so wet." Virginia groaned and arched her back, urging the older woman to slide her tongue into her tight slit.

Instead, Amelia reached up and tugged the hood of her clit back, giving it a few vicious tongue lashings, making her nearly scream and cry with please. "Don't tell me what to do, Ginny." She growled out at her, and Virginia quickly calmed and rested her hips on the ground as she whimpered and pouted.

I peered over to Amelia and furrowed my brow. "Components? Like what?" My fingers continue to press against my panties until I find myself slipping them beneath the fabric and rubbing directly. "Nn…"

"Your sweet cum." She cooed and shoved two fingers back inside Virginia's tight entrance. She cried out sharply and was moaning loudly as she was roughly fingered by the eager witch. "And somethin' of his. I know ya still got that scarf of his that he left in the barn durin' last winter's Circle." She giggled and slid up Virginia's body to rest her panty covered pussy on her face. "Start lickin', Ginny." She said softly. The young girl complied and began moving her head to slide her tongue along Amelia's panties. "Mm…"

I blushed darkly. She was right about the scarf and the sight before me didn't help the warm tingling all over my body. My legs were spread and my panties were tugged to the side now as I clearly stroked my fingers over my slick pussy. "I… I can do that." I managed out, shocked by my own willingness to try. "It would make him want me?"

She nodded and rocked her hips against Virgnia's face. By now, the young girl had tugged the panties aside and was eagerly lapping at her friend's pussy. "Mn! Yeah… he won't be able to take his hands off of ya." She grinned darkly at me.

I bit my bottom lip and started to pant. I was already close! So I kept going even more roughly and eagerly as I watched the leader of our group ride my poor, innocent friend's face. "A-alright…" I groan and arch my back.

I noticed as I did that, Amelia sighed in some annoyance and slipped off of Virginia, whose face was glistening and sticky. She licked at her lips and begin rubbing her clit as she tugged at her nipples individually as if trying to milk her huge breasts. "Don't cum yet!" Our resident witch hissed at me and grabbed a glass container from her bag. She held it right beneath my pussy and nearly purred at me it sounded like. "Mn, no. Squirt it all in here."

I looked at her hesitantly but was too aroused and curious to argue. I started to dip my hands between my pink lips and I toyed with an all too sensitive spot inside until I teetered over the edge. "Oh! God!" I cried out and came, squirting into the container like she told me to. I heard the lewd squishing sound and the little splash from it hitting the glass. My sticky cum dripped down the sides and some of it missed completely and got onto Amelia.

She didn't care at all, starting to lick her hand off. "Mn, good girl. We'll do it tomorrow afternoon. Isn't he comin' down with his family tomorrow evenin' to get some crops?" She gave me a wicked grin.

It was all happening so fast! I nodded and tugged my dress back down over myself. "Yeah, he is…"

"Then we'll see how well it works tomorrow!" She put a lid over the container and returned her attention to Virginia.

The rest of the night was kind of a blur. I know she made our friend climax at least ten times until she was exhausted and the hay beneath her was a sticky mess along with her thighs. Her nipples became raw and red and every little touch to the fabric of her dress made her whimper and moan in need. Something was definitely happening to us and Amelia was the only one who could control it. I should have told someone about what was going on with us, but I wanted the spell for Tyler to work. He never noticed me before and I doubt he ever would unless he was persuaded.

VI.

The next day, we all met in my family's barn in the early afternoon. I had brought the scarf in question from last night and set it down in front of Amelia. It seemed like Virginia hadn't gotten any new clothes yet because her dress barely contained her enlarged breasts and looked like they were squeezed almost painfully together. I could clearly see her erect nipples prodding at the fabric, threatening to burst out! I couldn't think of her like that, though! So I turned my attention to Amelia who was looking through the book already. "Is that all ya need?" I questioned with concern, hoping there wasn't much else to it. I didn't have anything else to give!

She looked over to me and nodded. "Yep. C'mon, let's sit in a circle."

Both Virginia and I did as she said and sat down in a small circle made of three. Virginia placed the scarf in the middle and took out the little glass container that had my arousal in it still.

I blushed and looked away as Amelia opened it and poured it over the scarf.

She took the book in her lap and settled on a page that looked rather... worn. Love spells like this must have been popular back then or something. "Alright, servants, hold hands." She grinned at both of us and laughed quietly.

I pursed my lips at her and narrowed my gaze, but Virginia smiled sheepishly and did as she was told. We all joined hands and leaned closer to each other.

Amelia cleared her throat and began chanting in foreign words that she couldn't possibly understand. At least, it would be incredible if she did. This was beginning to feel dangerous as I listened but held still. The chanting continued for at least five minutes and her voice grew stronger and louder. I was thankful that my parents were off visiting someone else's farm or they'd surely here Amelia carrying on! At the height of the ceremony, the scarf suddenly burst into flames and fizzled into ashes. Though we didn't meant to, both Virginia and I yelped and broke the circle.

Our witch friend laughed and leaned back. "You're lucky it was done. You might've ruined it or gotten us hurt, clumsy girls." She was already eyeing Virginia and had moved over to her. She began to kiss her deeply and tore her dress open easily from the front. Her fingers rubbed over the girls nipples and made her whimper and whine softly.

"Amelia! I... I can't... my nipples are so sore from last night." She insisted but tilted her head to kiss her again desperately in a messy way.

I heard a loud truck coming down to the road and gasped. Tyler and his family! "You two get out!" I snapped at them and tossed my shawl at Virginia so she could cover herself. "Hurry!"

Amelia got to her feet and helped the young girl up as well. "Oh, fine fine. You're lucky I did this for ya!" She leaned in and kissed me deeply, licking my lips playfully. "You'll have to tell me about it, Mary." She cooed, then left the barn quickly with Virginia and the book. I almost felt sorry for what may happen to the young girl tonight, but I was thinking more of what would happen for me.

VII.

Later that night after Tyler's parents dropped him off at my house to hang out, we ended up in the barn.

"Hey, Mary…" He was looking at me all night and was flushed. Actually, he looked aroused with how he breathed and panted lightly here and there.

"Yeah?" I murmured and sat closer to him in the hayloft.

He reached over and started to kiss on my cheek, even moaning just a little. "I've been trying to keep my hands off of you all night. But I can't. I don't know why but I need to feel you."

Was it working?! I grinned a little and nodded. "Do what ya want, Tyler." I spread my legs a little so that my dress hiked up to my thighs. I'd never been with a man before but I was so eager and rather confident.

"Farm girls are so slutty..." He smirked at me and then leaned in and kissed me rather roughly. His hand came up and began gripping my breasts, making them ache already. He then moved between my legs and lifted one up so that his middle touched to mine. As we kissed and moaned against each other, he began to thrust against me, rubbing the bulge of his jeans into my sticky panties.

"Oh! Ya feel so thick..." I groaned breathlessly and reached down to tug my panties to the side.

I immediately sat back and spread my legs wide to take a look at my pussy now. "Nng, fuck." He yanked my panties off and tossed them over the edge of the loft carelessly. Then he reached up and forced the top of my dress down with a tears. My breasts bounced free and he was immediately biting and sucking on them. His fingers quickly rubbed against my pussy and caused wet squishing sounds as he spread my arousal around and caused it to squirt a little when he pressed down roughly.

"Ah, y-you're so strong…" I gasped softly, arching my back as I enjoyed his firm touch. I rocked my hips in a way so his fingers would sometimes slip inside of my needy slit as he teased me.

"I know." He replied smugly. "I never thought of you like this before. But now… there's just something about you and it makes me so hard." He leaned back to show me the bulge in his jeans, making them tight. "It hurts.

You should take it out." He gave a toothy grin and placed one of my hands on the front of his pants.

I felt his cock throbbing beneath the fabric and I couldn't take it anymore. I grabbed it a little to feel it and I could tell already that it was big. I hastily unzipped his pants and yanked them down along with his boxer briefs. The length that sprung out had to be at least eight and a half inches and rather thick. I leaned forward and almost instinctively began to lick up the sides and to the head where I sucked softly. My tongue curiously found the pronounced ridge around his tip and I began to lap and slide my tongue around it.

It made him buck his hips and moan a bit loudly in need. Before I knew it, he had his hand on the back of my head and I was gagging on his cock in my throat. My eyes met his and he was grinning with smug satisfaction as he heard me gag and whimper against him. It was making for a messy blowjob, then he released me.

I gasped sharply and groaned, licking my lips. "Mn, it tastes so good." I panted out and leaned in to take more.

"No." He stopped me and pushed me back. "You got it wet and now I want you on your knees with your ass out." He kissed me firmly and then trailed his lips down my neck.

I knew exactly what he wanted, so I nodded and turned around. I almost fell to my side because I was so eager. I held onto a wooden rail in front of me and spread my knees apart wide. My pussy was dripping sticky arousal down to the floor and my thighs. I was more than ready for him to take me. I'd waited way too long for my first cock. "Will that thing fit?" I questioned, still a bit concerned because of how big he seemed.

"Heh, oh yeah. It'll fit." He assured me and I could feel his head rubbing against my lower lips firmly. He made sure to press hard enough that it was teasing terribly the thought and feel of penetration. It would flick up to my clit and back down to my entrance. Then he pushed hard and shoved balls deep inside of my cunt. "Shit! You really were a virgin." He laughed a little, quite pleased with himself. "So that makes you mine, doesn't it?" He placed his hands on both of my cheeks and gave one a firm slap to make it jiggle and bounce.

I cried out sharply and so loudly that my voice almost went hoarse. I bucked back against him, starting to fuck him before he could even move against me. "Y-yeah. I... mn! It hurts... you're stretchin' me, but it's so good!" I moaned loudly.

He moaned with me, more deeply and closer to grunts that my little whimpers and cries. "You'll fit me so perfectly after this, Mary!" He grinned. I could hear it in his voice. His hips picked up pace, and he was fucking my so hard that he shoved me up against the railing that I was holding onto.

Spell or not, this was amazing and I bet he'd come back for more. Now I had him whenever I wanted it. I almost felt bad for manipulating him like this, but maybe this was all he needed, anyway. A little magic didn't hurt, right? "I'm gonna cum!" I arched my back, moaning in need each time he hit that perfect spot inside of me when he hilted as deeply as he possibly could.

"Mn! Good! I'm gonna cum inside of you." He groaned and started to buck upward to lift my knees off of the ground each time. "Can't wait to see my cum dripping out of your little pussy."

I wasn't sure if this was how he acted normally during sex, but I couldn't really complain. A dark side of me loved this depraved act in my family's barn with a man that had no idea he was under the influence of Amelia's magic. I could feel myself tense up and throb over his thick length as it pounded me desperately in attempt to get me to cum before him. It worked before I squeezed him pleasantly as I came hard and squirted against his cock, only some of it dripping out from the tight seal he made inside of me. "Oh! Amazin'!"

He lost control and pounded into me without thought until he came hard. I felt his warm cum fill me up and move inside until he was forced to drip out, especially when he pulled back. He panted heavily and fell onto his knees. His cock was still hard and twitching as his cum ran down it and over his spent balls. "Shit, Mary…" He groaned and started to stroke his sensitive length. His body jerked a little as he touched himself.

After a moment, I composed myself and raised my hips up a little, using my fingers to spread my lips. I groan as I push and some of his seed out for him to see. "It's so much. Did ya really release that much?" I panted out.

He reached out and turned me around, kissing me deeply. "Mn… yeah. I haven't jerked it in days and you felt so good." He held my body against him and took my hand to start stroking him myself. He even remained hard!

I leaned against him and started to kiss lazily at his neck. "Can we do this more often? Would ya visit me?" I murmured curiously.

He nodded. "I'd be stupid to give up pussy like this." He grinned at me and nudged me. "And… I do like you. I don't know why we've never hung out outside of your city trips until now." As he spoke, he casually reached down between my legs and stroked his fingers along my messy slit. "I don't know what came over me this time."

It was almost too delicious to hear him talk like that. I knew exactly why he was here with me now, and I didn't care about the reason.